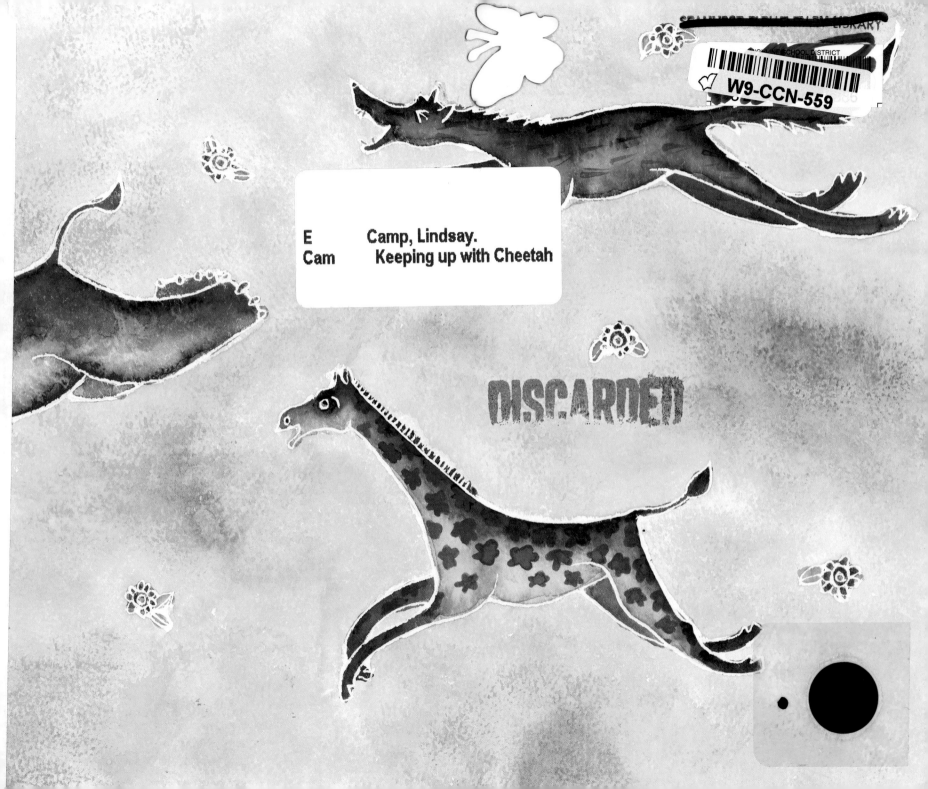

For Anna, who always laughs at my jokes.
Well, usually.
L.C.

To my young grandma, with love.
J.N.

Text copyright © 1993 by Lindsay Camp
Illustrations copyright © 1993 by Jill Newton
First published in Great Britain by All Books For Children

Printed in Hong Kong.

First U.S. Edition   1   2   3   4   5   6   7   8   9   10

Library of Congress Cataloging in Publication Data was not available in time for publication of this book,
but can be obtained from the Library of Congress.   Keeping Up With Cheetah.   ISBN 0-688-12655-3.
Library of Congress Catalog Card Number 92-44162

KEEPING UP WITH CHEETAH

by **LINDSAY CAMP**

illustrated by **JILL NEWTON**

LOTHROP, LEE & SHEPARD BOOKS   **NEW YORK**

Cheetah and Hippopotamus were friends. They liked to sit under a shady tree and tell each other jokes. Actually, it was Cheetah who told the jokes. Hippopotamus just listened and laughed—a deep, bellowy laugh. Cheetah's jokes weren't very funny, but Hippopotamus thought they were. And that's why they were such good friends.

Just one thing about Hippopotamus annoyed Cheetah—Hippopotamus couldn't run very fast.

"Come on, Hippopotamus," Cheetah would shout impatiently. "If you don't keep up with me, you won't hear my new joke."

It did no good. Hippopotamus simply couldn't run as fast as Cheetah. So Cheetah made friends with Ostrich instead. Hippopotamus felt like crying. Instead, he practiced running. He practiced and practiced, until he was so out of breath, he had to lie down.

But he still couldn't keep up with Cheetah.

Ostrich could—almost, anyway. Cheetah
was very pleased with his new friend. "Would
you like to hear my new joke, Ostrich?" he asked.

"No, thanks," said Ostrich. "I don't like jokes. Let's run some more."

Cheetah had done enough running for one day. Now he wanted to tell jokes. So he made friends with Giraffe instead. When Hippopotamus saw this, he was even more miserable—and even more determined to run as fast as Cheetah.

So he hid and watched very carefully as Giraffe
and Cheetah galloped by. Giraffe's long legs flew
out in front of her. Cheetah lashed his tail from
side to side to keep his balance.

Hippopotamus tried to do the same. It wasn't easy.
His legs didn't want to fly out in front, and his
tail was much too short to lash from side to side.

It looked like it might be a long
time before he could keep up with
Cheetah.

Giraffe could—almost, anyway.
Cheetah was very pleased
with his new friend.

"Would you like to hear my new joke, Giraffe?"
he asked. Giraffe didn't answer. "Giraffe! Would
you like to hear my new joke?"

"Pardon me?" said Giraffe. "I can't hear you very
well from up here."

Cheetah was cross. What good was a friend who
couldn't hear your best jokes?

So he made friends with Hyena instead. When
Hippopotamus saw this, he felt thoroughly
hot and bothered. There was only one thing
that would make him feel better: a good long wallow.

Hippopotamus loved to wallow. The deeper, the muddier, the better. And he hadn't had a wallow for a long time. Cheetah said it was dirty.

But if Cheetah didn't want to be friends anymore, Hippopotamus could do what he liked. He stomped down to the river and dived into the muddiest spot—SPLOOSH! It felt wonderful!

And as he lay there, Hippopotamus thought how silly he'd
been. He wasn't the right shape for running fast, but
he was exactly right for wallowing. And although he was
sad to lose a friend, he knew that, whatever he did, he
would never be able to keep up with Cheetah.

Hyena could—almost, anyway. Cheetah was very pleased with his new friend.

"Knock knock," said Cheetah.

"Ha-hee-he-heeee!" said Hyena.

"You're supposed to say 'Who's there?'" snapped Cheetah.
"What's the point of telling you my best new joke if
you laugh before I get to the funny part?"
"HAH-HEH-HEE-HEE-HEE!" screamed Hyena.

Cheetah was disgusted. He could run by himself, but telling jokes was no fun unless someone could hear you, and wanted to listen, and only laughed at the funny parts. Where could he find a friend like that?

He already had one! Cheetah ran to the shady tree, but Hippopotamus wasn't there. How silly he had been to lose such a good friend.

Suddenly he saw a pair of eyes watching him from the river.

"Would you like to hear my new joke?" asked Cheetah.

"All right," said Hippopotamus.

"Knock knock," said Cheetah.
"Who's there?" said Hippopotamus.
"H," said Cheetah.
"H who?" said Hippopotamus.
"H-eetah, of course!" said Cheetah.
 And Hippopotamus laughed and laughed.